hemist❖alchemy❖algebra❖align❖allegory❖alopecia❖amazement❖amber❖amethyst❖amuse❖anc... P9-BZL-758

rmadillo❖armlet❖armor❖army❖arrow❖asparagus❖astray❖astrolabe❖astronomer❖astronomy❖attempt❖awe❖awesome❖axe

bison❖bite❖black❖blue❖blush❖blushing❖boat❖bob❖bold❖bolt❖bone❖book❖bounce❖bounced❖bow❖boy❖brass❖bronze

amel❖camlet❖camouflage❖canary❖candelabra❖candle❖candlestick❖canister❖canopy❖canteen❖cape❖carrying❖carved

❖checkered❖cheese❖chef❖chest❖chestnut❖chimpanzee❖chipmunk❖chirp❖choice❖chortle❖chuckle❖circle❖clairvoyant❖claw

❖crab❖crack❖crazy❖crescent❖crest❖crimson❖crocodile❖cross❖crossbow❖crown❖crystal❖crystal ball❖curls❖curly❖cushion

gram❖dial❖diamond❖diaphanous❖dinner❖dinosaur❖dish❖dismay❖dividers❖dodo❖dome❖dome-headed❖dominoes❖donkey

❖dupe❖eagle❖ear❖earring❖earth❖east❖eat❖eccentric❖eclipse❖edge❖egg❖eggcup❖eggshell❖Egyptian❖eight❖elaborate

pe❖epaulet❖equator❖equinox❖err❖escape❖espadrilles❖exasperated❖exotic❖expedition❖exploration❖expression❖eye❖eyeball

❖fellow❖felt❖fence❖fez❖fin❖find❖finger❖fingernail❖fire❖fish❖fishing basket❖fishing line❖fishing rod❖fist❖five❖five-o'clock

❖florid❖flower❖fluffy❖flute❖fluttering❖flying❖folded❖folds❖follow❖foot❖footslogger❖force❖forearm❖forefinger❖forehead

❖full❖fulvous❖fur❖fusilier❖gabble❖gaggle❖gamekeeper❖gander❖gargantuan❖garment❖garnet❖garnish❖gash❖gate❖gauntlet

ider❖globe❖glove❖glum❖goanna❖goat❖go-between❖goblet❖goggles❖going❖gold❖golden egg❖goldfish❖gong❖goose❖gorilla

oscope❖hair❖halter❖hamster❖hand❖handkerchief❖handle❖hank❖happy❖harangue❖hare❖harp❖hat❖haversack❖hawking❖hawser

mus❖hive❖hoe❖hoist❖holding❖hole❖holler❖honeycomb❖honk❖hood❖hoof❖hook❖hoop❖hop❖horn❖horrified❖horse❖horseshoe

❖implement❖impossible❖imprison❖in❖Indian❖indigo❖individual❖inertia❖ingenious❖ingot❖initial❖ink❖innocent❖inscription

n-packed❖jape❖japer❖jar❖jaw❖jester❖jewel❖jewelry❖jigsaw❖jocose❖jocund❖jolly❖journey❖joust❖joyful❖jug❖juggle❖jute

ilt❖kiltie❖kind❖kindling❖king❖kingfisher❖kink❖kirtle❖kith❖kiwi❖knapsack❖knave❖knee❖knight❖knit❖knob❖knot❖knuckle

ladybird❖lag❖lamb❖lambent❖lament❖lamp❖lance❖lantern❖lap❖lapel❖lappet❖large❖lariat❖lashings❖lasso❖last❖latch❖latitude

❖lettering❖lever❖lid❖liege❖light❖lighthouse❖lightning❖lilac❖lime❖limn❖line❖linear❖link❖linkwork❖lion❖lip❖list❖little

np❖lurch❖luxuriant❖mace❖magenta❖magnet❖magnify❖magnifying glass❖magpie❖mail❖male❖mallet❖mammals❖mammoth

easuring tape❖medal❖medley of maps❖meeting❖melon❖memorable❖mend❖merciful❖message❖message in a bottle❖messy

❖moving❖music❖nab❖nail❖Napoleon Mouse❖Napoleonic❖narwhal❖nascent❖naught❖naughty❖near❖nebulous❖needle❖nest

s❖number❖nurse❖nurture❖oar❖oarsman❖oasis❖obelisk❖obfuscation❖object❖objects❖obligation❖oblique❖oblong❖obnoxious

r❖off-white❖ogle❖ogling❖oh❖old❖old-world❖olive❖one❖onions❖oops❖openmouthed❖opposition❖opt❖orange❖orangutan❖orb

padlock❖pail❖paint❖paintbrush❖pair❖paisley❖paletot❖pallor❖palm❖palm frond❖pan❖panda❖panel❖panic❖pantograph❖pants

culiar❖peep❖peer❖peg leg❖pelage❖pelican❖penalty❖pendant❖penguin❖penna❖pennant❖pennon❖perched❖peregrination❖peril

les❖pinion❖pink❖pinnacle❖piping❖pirate❖piscivorous pelican❖pitchfork❖plank❖pleat❖plight❖plug❖plumage❖plumate❖plumb

❖precarious❖preparation❖presiding❖prickly❖proboscis❖prod❖protest❖prow❖pull❖pumpkin❖punish❖punishment❖pupil❖puppet

❖quality❖qualms❖quandary❖quarrel❖quarry❖quarter❖quartet❖quartz❖quaver❖quay❖queen❖quell❖querulous❖query❖quest

on marks❖quotes❖rabbit❖rabble-rouser❖raccoon❖race❖racketeer❖radiating❖raft❖rag❖ragged❖raggedy❖rags❖raiment❖rain

g❖realm❖rear❖rebus❖reckless❖rectangle❖red❖red ribbon❖reed❖reef knot❖regal❖relic❖relief map❖relief motif❖remarkable

❖rising sun❖rivage❖river❖rivets❖rock❖rocking❖rodent❖rogue❖rope❖rose❖round table❖row❖rowing❖royal blue❖rubiginous

safe❖safeguard❖sagging❖sagittal❖sail❖sailor❖salient❖sallet❖sally forth❖saltire❖salute❖sand❖sandal❖sapphire❖sash❖saucepan

crewdriver❖scroll❖scrutiny❖scutcheon❖sea❖seaborne❖seafaring❖seagull❖seal❖seaman❖search❖seat❖see❖seeking❖selachian

oulder❖shovel❖shroud❖sideburns❖sight❖signal❖silly❖sinister❖sinking sailor❖sinking ship❖sisal❖sitting❖six❖skating❖skunk

nner❖spider❖spindrift❖spiral❖splash❖spots❖spray❖squall❖squares❖staircase❖stalwart❖stand❖stars❖stash❖staves❖steadfast

swashbuckling❖swinging❖sword❖symbol❖tablecloth❖tache❖taciturn❖tail❖talisman❖talons❖tame❖tan❖tankard❖target❖tartan

e❖thrilling❖through❖thumb❖tick❖tied❖tiger❖tight❖tigress❖tin❖tip❖toad❖toadstool❖toby jug❖toe❖toe cap❖toggle❖tongue

sure❖triangle❖tricky❖trumpet❖trumpeting❖tubular❖tulip❖tunic❖turkey❖turquoise❖twelve❖twenty❖twined❖twins❖twisted

ants❖undertaking❖underwear❖undone❖undulating❖uneven❖unfastened❖unfortunate❖unhappy❖unhook❖unicorn❖uniform

vegetable❖veil❖vent❖vermilion❖vertex❖vertical❖vertices❖vertigo❖vessel❖vest❖vested❖veteran❖vex❖viaduct❖vicinage

ute❖voyage❖vulture❖waders❖waist❖waistband❖waistcoat❖waistline❖waiting❖wale❖walk❖walking❖walkway❖wall-eyed

orks❖wave❖waver❖way❖wayfarer❖wayfaring❖wayward❖wealth❖wear and tear❖wearing❖weary❖weasel❖weathered

hatley❖wheat❖wheel❖wheelbarrow❖whet❖whim❖whimsical❖whiskers❖white❖wick❖wicker basket❖wickerwork

er❖wonderment❖wonderstruck❖wood❖woodborer❖wooden❖woof❖words❖working❖worm❖worthy❖wound❖woven

zebra❖zenith❖zeroed in❖zestful❖zig-zag❖zinnia❖zircon❖zodiac❖and many many more words for you to find

The arrow has been launched. . . .
The Alphabet Quest is on!

As you embark on your journey through the twenty-six letters of the alphabet, you will be on a quest for buried treasure. All kinds of adventures await you, but you must look carefully; this book rewards only the sharp-eyed and curious. Are you ready to accept the challenge? Well, then . . . let's begin!

Here are a few clues to help you on your way:

❖*Look for the hidden letters on each page. Some are easy to find, and some are cleverly tucked away, so don't give up. Good things come to those who look and look!*

❖*Hunt for all the animals and objects beginning with the same letter on each page. How many can you find? Some of the words are listed on the endpapers, but you can find many, many more.*

❖*Make up sentences from the words you find. Gorilla is glum as he touches the globe with his glove; what about Pirate Pig? How many words beginning with the same letter can you use in a single sentence?*

❖*Make up stories out of your sentences and out of the words you find. Follow these stories through the pages. Is Gorilla glum because Fox has filched a fragment of his treasure map? What happens to Horse? The stories and illustrations are continuous, but only you can find the words to connect them!*

❖*Discover the treasure waiting for you at your journey's end. Knowledge is the key, and with this key you can unlock the secret of the letters and use their magic forever!*

WHATLEY'S QUEST

WRITTEN BY
Bruce Whatley & Rosie Smith

ILLUSTRATED BY
Bruce Whatley

HarperCollinsPublishers

*For Mum whose love and perseverance gave me
the gift of my right arm. And for Dad ~a true craftsman.*
Bruce

For Mum with love and in loving memory of Dad.
Rosie

*For our children, Ben and Ellyn.
Thank you for your inspiration and patience.
May your aim be true.
Love from Mum and Dad*

First published in 1994 in Australia by Angus & Robertson,
an imprint of HarperCollins Publishers, 25 Ryde Road,
Pymble, Sydney, NSW 2073, Australia.

Whatley's Quest
Copyright © 1994 by Bruce Whatley
Concept by Rosie Smith and Bruce Whatley
Printed in the U.S.A. All rights reserved.
1 2 3 4 5 6 7 8 9 10
❖
First American Edition, 1995
ISBN 0-06-026291-5
ISBN 0-06-026292-3 (lib. bdg.)

Archer, *draw back your bow*
for you will direct our journey.

Our Quest~
the pursuit of knowledge
and the gathering of wisdom.

Archer, aim your arrow high,
and may your aim be true.

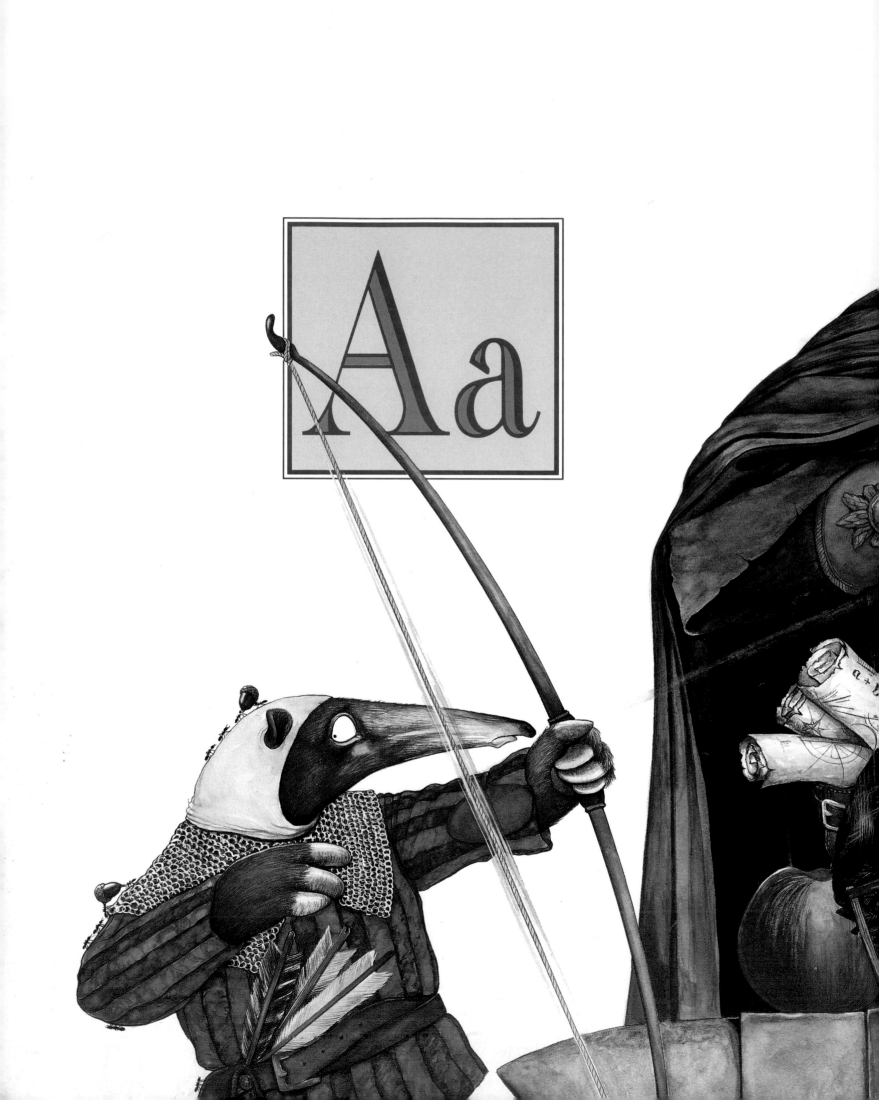

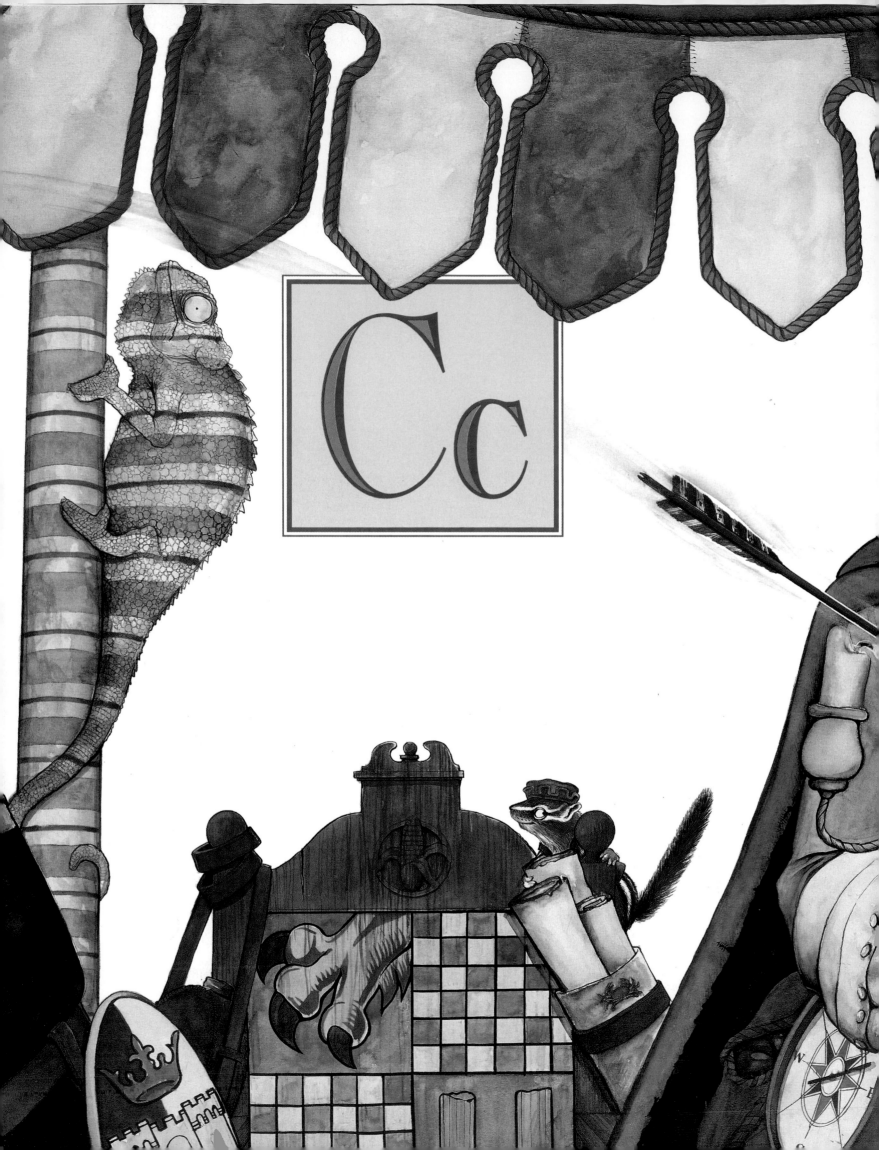

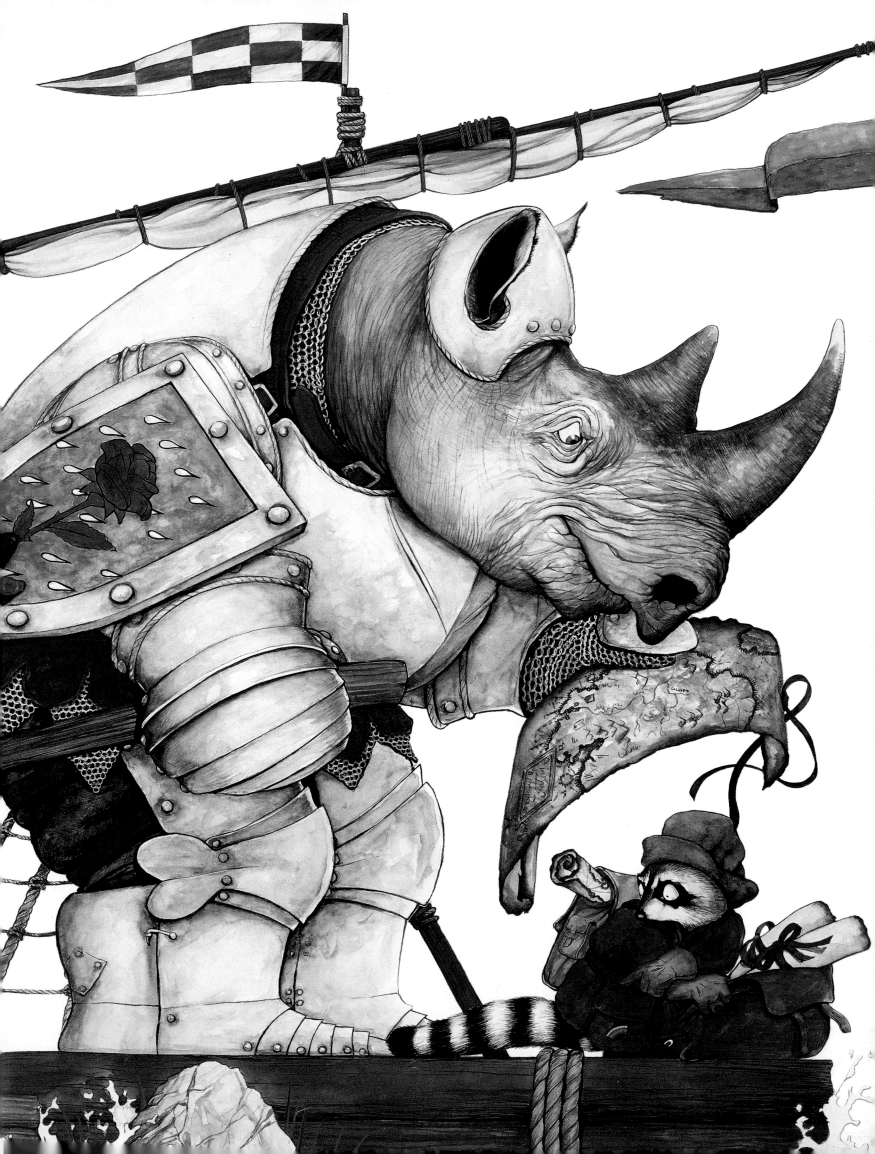

Xx Yy
Zz

Now it is your Quest…
Always aim your arrow high,
and may your aim be true.

abacus❖ability❖able❖above❖accident❖accountant❖accurate❖achieve❖acorn❖action❖add❖ ❖aim❖albatross❖
❖annoying❖answer❖ant❖antagonist❖anteater❖antique❖ants❖anvil❖anxious❖apple❖applique❖arc❖archer❖ardent❖arm❖
❖back❖bag❖ball❖banana❖banner❖baseball❖baseball glove❖basket❖bat❖beak❖bear❖behind❖bell❖belt❖beret❖big❖bill❖bir
brooding❖brown❖brown bear❖buffalo❖bull❖bullock❖bunting❖burly❖butterfly❖button❖buttonhole❖cage❖call❖calling
castellations❖castle❖caterpillar❖Celtic cross❖chain❖chair❖challenge❖chameleon❖champion❖character❖chartreuse❖charts❖ch
❖cloak❖cloudy❖cob❖cobweb❖collar❖column❖comet❖compass❖cone❖consult❖cook❖cord❖core❖corn❖corner❖coupe❖cou
❖dagger❖dais❖dame❖damsel❖danger❖day❖dazed❖dead❖decoy❖deduce❖deer❖defiant❖demand❖design❖device❖diagonal❖
❖dot❖doubtful❖down❖dozen❖dragon❖drake❖drape❖drawing❖dreadful❖dreaming❖drill❖drink❖drop❖drum❖drumstick❖d
elbow❖elegant❖elephant❖eleven❖elf❖embarrass❖emblem❖emerald❖empty❖emu❖encounter❖end❖ensign❖enterprise❖env
❖eyeballing❖eyeful❖eyesight❖fable❖fabric❖face❖facial❖faithful❖falcon❖falling❖fans❖fast❖fastening❖fat❖fawning❖feather❖fe
shadow❖fixated❖flag❖flag bearer❖flageolet❖flagman❖flags❖flagstone❖flame❖flat❖fletching❖flight❖flights❖floating❖flock
❖foresight❖fork❖forward❖foul deed❖four❖fowl❖fox❖fragile❖fragment❖frayed❖freckles❖free❖friend❖frill❖fringe❖frog❖fro
❖gawking❖gazing❖geese❖gem❖gentle❖geography❖gesture❖giant❖gift❖gigantic❖girdle❖girl❖girth❖give❖glance❖glaucous❖
❖gosh❖granny❖grapes❖grass❖grasshopper❖grate❖gray❖green❖grill❖grim❖grimace❖grip❖grooves❖ground❖guide❖guinea pig❖
❖hear❖hearts❖heavy❖helmet❖helping❖hen❖henna❖heraldry❖heron❖hexagon❖hiding❖hieroglyphics❖hiking❖hill❖hinge❖hippop
❖hourglass❖ibex❖ibis❖iceberg❖icon❖ideograph❖igloo❖iguana❖illustration❖image❖imago❖immure❖impact❖imperfect❖impin
insect❖inset❖inside❖intent❖intersect❖intricate❖intrigue❖involute❖iris❖irons❖irregular❖island❖italic❖ivy❖jack❖jacket❖jade❖
kaleidoscope❖kangaroo❖kayak❖keel❖keep❖keg❖kern❖kettle❖kettledrum❖key❖keyhole❖key ring❖keystone❖khaki❖kick❖kid❖
❖koala❖koan❖kudos❖label❖labor❖labyrinth❖lace❖lacerated❖laces❖lacing❖lackadaisical❖lacuna❖lad❖ladder❖laden❖ladle❖lad
❖lattice❖laugh❖lavender❖laying❖leaf❖lean❖leaping❖learn❖leather❖ledge❖left❖leg❖leggings❖lemon❖length❖lens❖leopard❖le
lively❖lizard❖load❖loaded❖lobster❖lock❖locket❖locks❖locus❖lolling❖long❖longitude❖look❖loop❖lounging❖love❖lucky❖
mandarin❖mango❖manhandle❖map❖maple leaf❖marble❖maroon❖mascot❖massif❖mast❖mastodon❖mauve❖maze❖measure❖
metal❖metric❖milestone❖military❖mitten❖mole❖moleskins❖monocle❖moon❖moose❖motif❖mound❖mountain❖mouse❖mo
net❖nightdress❖nightgown❖nightingale❖nine❖ninety❖noble❖nook❖noose❖north❖nose❖nostril❖notation❖notches❖notebook❖n
observe❖obstacle❖obstruct❖obverse❖obvious❖occupant❖occurrence❖ocher❖ochroid❖octagon❖octant❖octopod❖octopus❖odd❖o
❖ordeal❖ordinary❖orifice❖origami❖orle❖ornery❖ostrich❖outwit❖oval❖overbearing❖overcome❖ovoid❖owl❖pace❖pack❖padd
❖paper❖parallel❖parcel❖parchment❖parody❖parrot❖part❖passenger❖passing❖patch❖patchwork❖paunch❖paw❖pawn❖pearls❖
❖periphery❖perplexed❖personnel❖persuade❖pettitoes❖pewter❖pi❖pick❖pickax❖pied❖pier❖pig❖piglet❖pigtail❖pillars❖pinea
❖plumb bob❖plumb line❖plummet❖plumose❖plunder❖plunger❖pocket❖point❖poke❖pole❖polka dots❖porky❖port❖pose❖p
❖puppy❖purple❖purposeful❖push❖quad❖quadrangle❖quadrant❖quadrate❖quadrilateral❖quadruped❖quadruplet❖quail❖quai
question mark❖queue❖quibble❖quiet❖quiff❖quill❖quilt❖quilted map❖quintain❖quintuplet❖quiver❖quizzical❖quoits❖quot
rainbow❖rainproof❖rake❖ram❖ramification❖rampart❖rapids❖rapt❖rascal❖rash❖rasp❖ratiné❖ratline❖rattle❖ray❖reaction❖rea
repair❖repine❖resting❖retard❖reverberate❖rhinoceros❖rhombus❖riant❖ribbon❖ricochet❖ridiculous❖rigging❖right❖ring❖risi
❖ruby❖rucksack❖rudder❖ruin❖ruminant❖rump❖rung❖running❖rush❖rushes❖russet❖rust❖sable❖sack❖sad❖saddle❖sad sack
❖save❖saw❖sawfish❖scabbard❖scalawag❖scan❖scarf❖scarlet❖scatterbrain❖scheming❖science❖scissors❖scoop❖screen❖screw
semaphore❖semicircle❖sentient❖serpent❖set of sails❖seven❖sextant❖shark❖sharp❖shells❖shelter❖shield❖ship❖shirt❖shoe
sky❖sleeve❖slipping❖slow❖sly❖smell❖smile❖snake❖snout❖snow❖snow leopard❖snow cloud❖sock❖sortie❖south❖spade❖s
steeve❖stench❖stern❖stink❖stitches❖stitching❖store❖stouthearted❖stow❖straps❖stubble❖stud❖sun❖surf❖surfing❖survey❖swa
❖task❖tassel❖taunt❖taut❖team❖teapot❖tear❖teasing❖telescope❖ten❖tethered❖texture❖thimble❖thistle❖thorn❖thorny❖threat❖t
toot❖torch❖torn❖torque❖tortoise❖toucan❖tourists❖tow❖toward❖towards❖tower❖towrope❖trail❖transit❖travelers❖traveling❖t
two❖umbrage❖umbrella❖unbearable❖unbolt❖unbuttoned❖unceremonious❖uncork❖uncovered❖under❖underarm❖underline❖und
united❖unlock❖unlucky❖unruffled❖up❖uphold❖uplift❖upon❖upset❖upside-down❖upstream❖upturn❖valiant❖valley❖varied❖vas
vicinity❖Viking❖vim❖vincible❖vine❖viola❖violate❖violence❖violet❖violin❖virtuous❖vitality❖vixen❖volant❖volcano❖volitant
❖walnut❖walrus❖wandering❖want❖ward❖warm-hearted❖warp❖watch❖watching❖water❖waterborne❖waterfall❖watering can❖wat
web❖wee❖weft❖weight❖weighty❖well❖well-balanced❖well-being❖wending❖west❖westering❖westwards❖wet❖whale❖wharf❖
❖wide❖will❖willing❖willy-nilly❖wily❖ ❖ ❖ ❖ e❖wisp❖wizard❖woebegone❖wolf❖wombat❖wo
❖wrinkles❖wrist❖writing❖xeric❖x-ray❖ ❖ ❖ ❖yarn❖yellow❖yes❖yoke❖youthful❖zany❖zealot